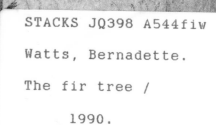

Ask your bookseller for these other North-South books
illustrated by Bernadette Watts:

The Elves and the Shoemaker by Jacob and Wilhelm Grimm
The Four Good Friends by Jock Curle
Goldilocks and the Three Bears retold by Bernadette Watts
The Little Donkey by Gerda Marie Scheidl
Mother Holly by Jacob and Wilhelm Grimm
The Ragamuffins by Jacob and Wilhelm Grimm
Shoemaker Martin by Leo Tolstoy
The Snow Queen by Hans Christian Andersen
Snow White and Rose Red by Jacob and Wilhelm Grimm
Tattercoats by Bernadette Watts

First published in the United States, Great Britain, Canada,
Australia and New Zealand in 1990 by North-South Books,
an imprint of Nord-Süd Verlag AG, 8625 Gossau Zürich, Switzerland

Library of Congress Catalog Card Number: 89-43730
British Library Cataloguing in Publication Data is available.
ISBN 1-55858-093-X

1 3 5 7 9 10 8 6 4 2
Printed in Belgium

The Fir Tree

HANS CHRISTIAN ANDERSEN

ADAPTED AND ILLUSTRATED BY

BERNADETTE WATTS

NORTH-SOUTH BOOKS

NEW YORK

In a lovely corner of the forest there grew a tiny fir tree, surrounded by many other trees, older and taller. The little fir tree had one wish: to be tall. It did not enjoy the sunshine or the fresh breeze.

It was not happy when children played around it, searching for wild strawberries. Often they gathered a whole basketful, then sitting down to rest would say, "What a pretty little tree!" which angered the fir tree.

The next year it was a little taller, the next taller still.

"If I were as tall as other trees," sighed the little tree, "I could see far over the world. Birds would build their nests in my branches; I would bow grandly in the wind."

When the forest lay deep in snow, a hare would run by and leap over the tree, much to the tree's annoyance. But after two winters it was too tall and the hare had to run round it. "Oh, to grow! To be old and tall!" the fir tree wished.

In autumn the tallest trees were felled. The fir tree shuddered as they crashed to the ground. Their branches were stripped off, so they hardly looked like trees at all. Then they were hauled away on wagons. Where were they going? What would happen?

In spring, when the swallows and storks arrived, the fir tree asked if they had met them. A stork nodded and said: "As I flew home from Egypt I met many ships with tall masts. They smelt like fir trees."

"Oh, to be tall enough to sail the seas!" said the tree.

"Rejoice in your young life!" said the sunbeams.

Christmas was coming! Many young fir trees, not as tall or old as our fir tree, were felled. They kept their branches and were taken away on carts. Our fir tree longed to travel away with the others.

"We know where they are going! We know!" twittered the sparrows. "We have peeped in the windows in the distant town and seen them planted in warm rooms and decorated with lovely things —apples, sweets, toys, and lighted candles. They enjoy the greatest respect."

The fir tree trembled with excitement. "Am I destined for such a life? If only it were Christmas! To be in that warm room, so grand and splendid! And something better must surely follow, or why do they decorate us so richly?"

"Be happy in your youth and freedom," said the wind.

But the fir tree could not be happy.

Throughout the year the fir tree grew and when Christmas came again it was the first to be felled. The axe struck deep and the tree felt such great pain it could no !onger think of grandeur. Suddenly it was sad to leave its home, its companions the bushes, flowers, birds.

The tree did not recover till it was unloaded in a back yard and heard a man say: "What a splendid tree!"

It was carried into a large room where there was a stove. Picture books and playthings lay on a table. The tree was placed in a tub of sand, draped with a green cloth. Then some young women hung its branches with gilded apples, nets of sugar plums and nuts, dolls, toys, and dozens of candles. At the top was fixed a golden star. "The candles will be lit tonight," said the women.

Night came at last! When the candles were lit, they shone so brightly that the tree trembled with delight, dazzled by its own finery. The door was thrown open and a crowd of excited children rushed in; the grown-ups followed sedately. For one moment the children stood in silence. Then, shouting and laughing, they rushed to the fir tree and tore off all the presents. The fir tree gasped with alarm. It was nearly knocked down, but no one cared about that. A grown-up peered among the branches for anything left, and then snuffed out all the candles.

"Tell us a story!" shouted the children, and pulled a little man to sit down by the tree.

"Now we are in the greenwood and the tree itself can listen," said the man. "I shall tell you about Humpty-Dumpty who fell downstairs, but was raised to glory and married a princess."

"Shall I have a part?" wondered the tree. But the tree had already played out its part.

When everyone had left, the fir tree stood, silent and thoughtful.
Never had it heard such a wonderful tale, not even from the birds in
the forest.

"Humpty-Dumpty fell downstairs, yet he married a princess,"
thought the tree. "If that is how things happen in the world, then so
it will be for me. I will be splendid again and marry a princess."

But in the morning the tree was dragged from the beautiful
room, up some stairs, and thrown into a dark attic.

The fir tree leaned sadly in a corner. Long days passed. No one came. The tree told itself, "It is winter now and I cannot be planted. The kind people are keeping me safely here till spring. But it is so lonely and dark!"

The tree remembered the forest, how pretty it was when the snow fell. It even remembered with pleasure how the hare would leap over it.

Some little mice visited the tree. "It would be quite comfortable here were it not so bitterly cold," squeaked one mouse. "Don't you think so, you old fir tree?"

"I am not old!" said the fir tree.

The inquisitive mice asked: "Have you been into the pantry—the most beautiful place in the world where cheeses lie on the shelves and hams hang from the ceiling?"

"I do not know that place," replied the tree, "but I know the forest where the sun shines and the birds sing."

The mice listened eagerly as it told them of its youth.

"How fortunate you were!" they squeaked.

Then the tree told them about Christmas Eve when it had been decorated.

"Oh, what a happy life you had!" cried the mice. "And you tell such wonderful stories!"

The next night more mice came and the night after that they brought along two rats. The more tales the tree told, the more clearly it recalled everything.

"Those happy days may return," it declared, "and, like Humpty-Dumpty, I may marry a princess." And it recalled a lovely birch tree in the forest, which to the fir tree was a princess.

The mice and rats listened to the story of Humpty-Dumpty.
"Very boring!" declared the rats. "Do you only know that story?"

"Only that one," said the fir tree. "I heard it on the happiest
evening of my life. I never knew then how happy I was."

"Well, we have heard quite enough, thank you," said the rats.
"We like stories about bacon and tallow-candles." Suddenly, the
mice no longer cared to listen either. They returned to their own
friends and left the tree alone.

One morning some people came to tidy the attic. They dragged out the fir tree and threw it downstairs.

"Now my life will begin again!" the fir tree thought, rejoicing in the sunshine and fresh air. It was thrown among weeds and nettles, but close by beautiful roses hung over a trellis, there were fragrant lime trees, and swallows flew about.

"I can breathe again!" And the tree spread out its branches; but alas! they were all dry and yellow. The gold star, still fixed to the treetop, glittered in the sunshine.

Some children were playing in the garden; the same children who had danced around the fir tree on Christmas Eve and thought it so beautiful.

"Look at the ugly old fir tree!" shouted the youngest. He trampled and snapped its branches, and tore off the gold star. The tree looked at the boy and the beautiful garden. Then it looked at itself, and wished it had remained hidden in the attic. It thought of its happy youth; the wonder of Christmas Eve; the friendly mice. "If only I had been happy when I could," it thought.

The gardener chopped the tree into pieces, which burned brightly when they were put on the fire. The children stopped playing to look at the fire. The branches sighed and cracked as if the heart of the tree were breaking.

With every crack the tree thought of a summer day in the forest or a winter night with stars shining brightly; it thought of Christmas Eve; it thought of the history of Humpty-Dumpty.

And so the fir tree was burned to ashes. The children played on and the youngest wore the gold star which the tree had worn on the happiest day of its life....

But that had all ended, and the story is ended, and that's the way with all stories.